CLASSIC STARTS™

# The Hunchback of Notre-Dame

*Retold from the Victor Hugo original*
*by Deanna McFadden*

*Illustrated by Lucy Corvino*

STERLING

New York / London
**www.sterlingpublishing.com/kids**

STERLING and the distinctive Sterling logo
are registered trademarks of Sterling Publishing Co., Inc.

**Library of Congress Cataloging-in-Publication Data**

McFadden, Deanna.
  The hunchback of Notre Dame / retold from the Victor Hugo original ;
abridged by Deanna McFadden ; afterword by Arthur Pober ; illustrated
by Lucy Corvino.
    p. cm.—(Classic starts)
  Summary: An abridged retelling of the tale, set in medieval Paris, of Quasimodo,
the hunchbacked bellringer of Notre Dame Cathedral, and his struggles to save
the beautiful gypsy dancer Esmeralda from being unjustly executed.
  ISBN-13: 978-1-4027-4575-1
  ISBN-10: 1-4027-4575-3
  1.  France—History—Medieval period, 987–1515—Juvenile fiction.
[1. France—History—Medieval period, 987–1515—Fiction. 2. Notre-Dame
de Paris (Cathedral)—Fiction. 3. People with disabilities—Fiction. 4. Paris
(France)—Fiction.] I. Corvino, Lucy, ill. II. Hugo, Victor, 1802–1885.
Notre-Dame de Paris. III. Title.

PZ7.M4784548Hun 2008
[Fic]—dc22

                                                                2007009218

2  4  6  8  10  9  7  5  3  1

Published by Sterling Publishing Co., Inc.
387 Park Avenue South, New York, NY 10016
Copyright © 2008 by Deanna McFadden
Illustrations copyright © 2008 by Lucy Corvino
Distributed in Canada by Sterling Publishing
$^c$/$_o$ Canadian Manda Group, 165 Dufferin Street,
Toronto, Ontario, Canada M6K 3H6
Distributed in the United Kingdom by GMC Distribution Services,
Castle Place, 166 High Street, Lewes, East Sussex, England BN7 1XU
Distributed in Australia by Capricorn Link (Australia) Pty. Ltd.
P.O. Box 704, Windsor, NSW 2756, Australia

Classic Starts is a trademark of Sterling Publishing Co., Inc.

*Printed in China*
*All rights reserved*

Sterling ISBN-13: 978-1-4027-4575-1
ISBN-10: 1-4027-4575-3

For information about custom editions, special sales, premium and
corporate purchases, please contact Sterling Special Sales
Department at 800-805-5489 or specialsales@sterlingpub.com.

# CONTENTS

# CHAPTER 1

# A Day of Celebrations

On the sixth of January, 1482, the city of Paris woke up to the ringing of bells. There were two celebrations going on that day: the Epiphany and the Festival of Fools. The Epiphany was a religious holiday. But the Festival of Fools was for the people. It was an annual celebration where everyone was expected to have fun. There would be fireworks, a May tree celebration, and a play at the Great Hall.

Most of the city's important men were going to see the play. All the streets leading to the Great

Hall were crowded with people who were talking and laughing as they walked along.

The long wait had made the crowd rowdy, and they complained about everything.

Like water that overflows, the crowd swelled as it swept around the pillars, filling every nook and cranny. People sat on windowsills, on sculptures—anywhere they could fit.

A group of students had knocked some glass out of a window and were boldly sitting on the sill. The young boys joked and laughed.

"Why, it's you, Joannes! How long have you been here?" one of them yelled to a handsome blond boy who was sitting on top of a sculpture in the middle of the room.

Joannes answered, "How do you do, Jehan Frollo? Your arms and legs are spinning like a windmill—is that how you're keeping balance on that windowsill? How long have we been here? More than four hours!"

2

The boys, who were bored with waiting, began to tease many of the important men in the crowd. They called them names and made fun of their hats, their jobs, their clothes. Anything they *could* laugh at, they *did* laugh at!

Then, at last, the clock struck twelve. "Ah!" the crowd said. The students grew silent, and the rest of the room settled down. Every neck was outstretched, every eye fixed on the stage, but there was nothing to be seen except the four bailiffs who were there to keep order, standing as stiff as statues.

The crowd waited one minute, two minutes, five, ten, and then they started chanting, "The play! The play!"

"Grab the bailiffs!" the students called. The crowd applauded, and the four men on stage turned quite pale. As the mob started toward them, the curtains flew open. A shaking actor emerged and walked to center stage.

"T-t-today we have the honor of performing *The Good Judgment,* a play by Pierre Gringoire. I will be playing Jupiter. The moment the cardinal arrives, we shall begin."

When everyone heard that there would be more waiting, they started shouting again.

"Begin right now!" Joannes shouted louder than anyone.

"Down with Jupiter! Down with the cardinal!" Jehan yelled.

Poor Jupiter started to slowly move off the stage. Just before he opened the curtains, a figure dressed in black emerged from backstage and whispered, "Hey, you, Jupiter!"

Jupiter took another step backward. "Who calls me?" The poor fellow spun around.

"It's me, Pierre," the playwright said quietly. "Start the play and I'll make sure the cardinal understands."

"O-okay." Jupiter nodded, and then turned

back around to face the audience. "We shall begin!"

The crowd whistled and cheered as the music started. It was perfectly quiet now in the Great Hall. The audience was awed by the actors' costumes: white and gold robes, each made from a different material—silk, linen, wool, and cotton.

Pierre stood back and watched the actors speak his words. The crowd had clapped at the beginning, and they were still watching. Those were good signs. But his happy mood did not last. An old beggar, dressed in rags with a large cut on his arm, wandered into the Great Hall. Jehan noticed him and called out, "Look at that sad sack up there!"

Every single eye in the room turned to look at the dirty man and stopped watching the play. The actors just stood there, not saying anything at all. The beggar looked around and said, "Spare change, if you please."

"Why," Joannes said, "it's old Clopin. I see your leg is better. It's your arm that's hurt now, is it?"

"Why are you stopping? Carry on!" Pierre whispered to the actors. And so they carried on even while people passed coins to the old beggar. Finally, the crowd settled down to watch the play again. It was perfect! Until the door just behind the stage flew open and the usher announced, "The Cardinal de Bourbon!"

*The noisy students are bad enough,* Pierre thought, *but now the cardinal interrupts my play as well!* It wasn't that he disliked Cardinal de Bourbon. He was simply upset that the crowd had once again turned away from the play to see what was going on.

Everyone wanted to get a better view of the important man. They peered over one another's shoulders, strained their necks, stood on tiptoes—anything to get a good look at the popular cardinal as he bowed to the audience and walked to his seat.

The students called out to the line of bishops behind him as they, too, took their seats. They were enjoying the Festival of Fools. It was the one day of the year when the students ruled the streets, joking, laughing, and causing trouble, all without much consequence.

The usher announced the Duke of Austria, and forty-eight men came in with him! The poor fellow had to call out each of their names and titles as the men took their seats. All of the men looked the same, with black velvet caps and still faces. A man with a jolly face and a funny leather vest, which looked odd in the sea of velvet and silk, tried to enter with the duke.

The usher stopped him. "You can't come in this way."

The man in the leather vest said, "I am Jacques Coppenole, tailor to the duke."

The usher was upset. His voice was hoarse from

calling out so many names, and this wasn't even a nobleman. "Monsieur Jacques Coppenole, tailor."

The gallery was now full to the brim with important people. Pierre had tried desperately to keep the play going during all of the entrances, but with little success. At last, though, it seemed that everyone was settled.

Pierre shook his head. He covered his mouth and yelled as loudly as he could, "Start the play! Come on, let's start the play!"

"What in the devil is going on?" Jehan said, "We've already seen half the play and they want to start it all over again? We'll not have that, will we?"

The cardinal asked the bailiff what the racket was about, and the bailiff explained that the play had already started.

The cardinal laughed and shouted, "Just tell them to keep going. It makes no difference."

*My play is ruined,* Pierre thought. *Now half the audience will know what's happening and the other half won't. It's a disaster!*

Then, to make matters worse, Jacques Coppenole stood up and started speaking. "Great people of Paris, what are we doing here? Do we call this a play? Why, there's not even any fighting! We were promised a Festival of Fools. What do you say? Down with the play and let's begin the Theater of Grimaces. We must find the man who can make the ugliest face and crown him Pope of Fools."

Pierre wanted to say something, but he was too angry to move. And to add insult to injury, the crowd seemed to love the idea. Now not a single person was interested in the play. They all had their minds set on choosing a Pope of Fools.

# CHAPTER 2

# The Pope of Fools

In the blink of an eye, everyone started to carry out Coppenole's idea. Townsmen, students, and lawyers all went to work. The little chapel inside the Great Hall was chosen as the place for the Theater of Grimaces. Two barrels were placed underneath the window the students had broken. The candidates were to stand on the barrels and look through the window with their faces covered. When they had frowned, scowled, or sneered as best they could, they would remove the covering and show their face to the audience.

In a few minutes, the chapel was full of people who wanted to compete. The first person stood on top of the barrel, put his head through the window, and uncovered his face. He was squinting and wrinkling his forehead; his eyes bulged out. The crowd roared with laughter.

Imagine the silliest faces people can make— well, that's what each one did as they stood on the barrels. No one stayed in their seats. Everyone howled and hooted. With each new face that came through the window, the laughter grew. Soon everyone in the crowd was making faces— posing as much as the person up on the barrel!

Jehan sat atop a statue and watched everything. He laughed so hard he almost fell over!

Meanwhile, poor Pierre was pacing backstage. The actors had stopped the play completely because they, too, were watching the fun.

*Poetry,* he thought, *is no match for comedy.*

At that very moment, the ugliest of ugly faces

made its way through the frame. The man had a mouth like a horseshoe, a large, triangular nose, a horny lip with a jagged tooth sticking out, one bushy red eyebrow, and one eye covered by a wart.

Here was the winner! The crowd rushed into the chapel only to find that the person was not making a face at all — he was just that ugly. On his back was a giant hump. His hair was nothing but red bristles. His legs were strangely put together and two different sizes, and his feet were huge. But despite looking so terrible, the man had an air of strength and courage about him.

"It's Quasimodo!" someone called. "The bell ringer."

"Look at his hunchback!" one of the students yelled. "He's terribly ugly, indeed!"

The students teased him, and the women covered their faces. Joannes walked right up to Quasimodo and laughed in his face, pointing and calling him names. Quasimodo picked him up and tossed him back into the crowd. He didn't like it when people teased him. He didn't understand that it was the Festival of Fools, and that the students were just having a bit of fun. Luckily, Joannes wasn't hurt. He stood up, brushed himself off, and laughed.

Coppenole, the tailor, was amazed to find that Quasimodo was so strong. He pushed himself forward and clapped his hand on the hunchback's shoulder. "You've got quite the arm there!"

Quasimodo didn't stir.

"I said," Coppenole continued, "you must be very strong. How do you feel about wrestling? What do you say?"

Quasimodo didn't answer him.

An old woman from the crowd shouted, "The bells have made him deaf."

"Well, he's the perfect ugly and deaf Pope of Fools," Coppenole said. "Does he speak?"

"He can speak when he likes," the old woman replied.

"Then we hereby crown you the Pope of Fools. Congratulations!" said Coppenole.

Coppenole placed the silver robe of the Pope of Fools over Quasimodo's back. The crowd hushed for a moment as the students raised him up on their shoulders. Quasimodo smiled when he looked down and saw all the straight, handsome, well-shaped men and women. The students carried him up and out into the streets of Paris for a parade.

Meanwhile, Pierre forced the actors to continue with the play. He didn't think everyone would leave, but in the blink of an eye the room was nearly empty. Oh, there were a few old men and women left behind. Some of the students had stayed atop the window, where they could watch the play, if it interested them, or look out at the parade. Pierre tried to convince himself that was good enough.

"It's Esmeralda!" one of the students called suddenly from the window. "Esmeralda is in the square."

At this, everyone in the Great Hall abandoned the play completely and moved to the windows. The play came to another crashing halt. Again, Pierre urged his actors to continue.

"We can't," Jupiter said.

"Why not?" Pierre hissed.

"The students have run off with the ladder. They wanted to climb up and see what's happening in the square."

This was the final blow. "These Parisians!" Pierre muttered to himself. "They come to see a play and then refuse to watch it. Who is this Esmeralda? And why is she ruining my play?"

CHAPTER 3

# The Poet and the Gypsy Girl

ᴄ◠ᴏ

Pierre was glad it was dusk when he left the Great Hall. The dark streets would hide him well as he tried to find a place to think quietly. Too upset to go back to his room, he walked the streets of the city. As the Pope of Fools parade came toward him, Pierre turned and ran the other way.

The streets were full of people lighting fire-crackers and sparklers, but the farther he walked, the emptier they became. The riverbank was unpaved, and soon he was up to his ankles in mud. Pierre walked almost to the edge of the city.

He looked across the river and saw a glimmer of light on the small island across the way.

A giant firecracker exploded, and Pierre sighed.

*Even the ferrymen are celebrating,* he thought. *I might as well join them.*

At night, all one could see from the river was the jagged outline of the buildings that made up the city's main square. Rows of narrow, gloomy houses spread out in the other three directions. In the middle of the square sat the stocks.

By the time Pierre reached the square, he was numb with cold. He had tried a shortcut, but had gotten caught in the windmills, which splashed him and soaked his cloak. A large crowd of people had formed a circle around a bonfire, and Pierre quickly walked over. But he couldn't get through.

"Oh, these people," he said to himself. "Can't they see that my shoes are leaking and my cloak is soaking wet?"

In fact, when he looked around, it seemed that

many of the people didn't need to get warm at all—they were just watching a girl dancing by the fire. Pierre could not decide if this girl was a fairy, an angel, or a human being. She was not tall, but she looked it because she was so slim. She had dark hair, flashing dark eyes, and pale skin. She danced and turned on an old carpet thrown under her feet. No one could take their eyes off her. Her arms were up above her head as she moved in

time with the tambourine. She spun and spun; her skirt swirled and swirled.

As Pierre looked around, he saw thousands of faces. One man watched the girl very closely. He was older, with only a few wisps of gray hair on his bald head. He was dressed like a priest with a long black cloak. Pierre watched this man while the girl danced. For some reason, the priest seemed familiar.

"Djali!" the girl said, and a pretty little white goat stood up. "It's your turn!"

The girl and the goat did some tricks. Djali showed the audience the date by banging her hoof on the tambourine. Then the girl asked Djali what time it was. The goat answered with seven strong kicks just as the clock in the square struck that exact time!

"There is witchcraft in this!" the priest called. The girl turned her back to him and bowed as the crowd clapped. Then she and the goat continued their act.

"The church would not be happy with this!" the priest cried.

The girl smiled and collected the coins that were offered to her. She stopped in front of Pierre and waited. Sweat fell from his brow. His fingers searched his empty pockets.

"Get out of here, you dirty gypsy!" called the voice of an old woman nearby. Scared, the girl turned away from the awful woman. Pierre couldn't stop staring at her. She started singing, and the strange, sweet song filled his ears. The music brought tears to his eyes as he listened to her birdlike voice.

The same woman yelled again, "I said be quiet, gypsy girl!"

The spell was broken, and Pierre's stomach grumbled. Just then, the Pope of Fools parade marched into the square. The long snake-like line of people had grown since they had left the Great Hall. Quasimodo sat on a throne carried by the students, including Joannes and Jehan. All kinds of music came from the parade: horns, tambourines, flutes, and voices. The hunchback smiled at the people lining the streets, feeling joy for the first time in his life. He didn't realize that it was all a joke.

Suddenly the priest pushed his way through the crowd and snatched the crown from Quasimodo's head.

"Wait!" Pierre said, "I know that man. It's Claude Frollo, the Archdeacon of Notre-Dame. What is he doing?"

Quasimodo jumped off the chair, and it crashed to the ground. Shrieks of terror came from the crowd. With one giant step, the hunchback was in front of the priest. He looked at him with his one eye and fell to his knees. Frollo pulled off Quasimodo's silver cloak and threw his cardboard wand to the ground. The two spoke to each other with their hands. When they finished, Frollo tapped Quasimodo's shoulder. He stood up as straight as he could on his crooked legs and followed the priest.

The students just stared at him. "That's my brother," Jehan whispered to Joannes. "Always spoiling the fun."

Their pope gone, the students wandered off in search of more entertainment.

"That was amazing!" Pierre said. "I've never seen a man jump like that—he landed so close to Claude Frollo, that Quasimodo!" The poet shook his head. "Now, where shall I find supper?"

Pierre decided to follow the gypsy girl. *Maybe she'll share her supper with me,* he thought. *If I can find the courage to talk to her, that is.*

# CHAPTER 4

# Pierre Follows Esmeralda

⌒⌢

Paris was shutting down for the night. Stores were closing, and shopkeepers were heading home. The streets were dark and deserted. Pierre followed the gypsy through lanes and alleys.

*At least she knows the way,* Pierre thought, *because I am certainly lost.*

After a while, the girl saw that he was following her. She stopped for a moment to turn and look at him. Pierre felt bad, so he slowed down and counted the cobblestones under his feet.

Suddenly he heard screaming! Racing around the corner, he found two men trying to carry the gypsy girl away.

"Stop that right now!" Pierre shouted. One of the men turned. It was Quasimodo! He took a quick step toward Pierre and pushed him with all his might. The poet fell to the ground and was knocked out cold. Quasimodo picked up the gypsy girl and started to carry her off as if she weighed nothing at all. But before he could get away, members of the King's Guard came charging up on their horses.

"Put that girl down!" the captain shouted as he ripped Esmeralda from the hunchback's arms and lifted her onto his horse. The soldiers leaped off their horses and tried to hold Quasimodo, who fought as hard as he could. The other man with Quasimodo disappeared before the captain's men could catch him.

"Are you all right, miss? It's a good thing the King's Guard was here. My name is Captain Phœbus."

"Fine, thank you, kind sir," she said as she slipped off the horse. Before Captain Phœbus could say anything else, she, too, sped off into the night.

"Let's take him to the jail," Captain Phœbus said. "They can punish him tomorrow." The guards rode off with poor Quasimodo in tow.

Meanwhile, Pierre lay on the cobblestones. The painful chill of the ground finally woke him up. When he opened his eyes, he found himself in the gutter.

He thought for a moment about what had happened. There was another man with the hunchback, but who could it have been?

Pierre gasped when he realized the answer. Claude Frollo, the archdeacon! Why did he want to take the young gypsy girl?

"My goodness!" Pierre shouted. "It's cold!"

The mud in the gutter was stealing the heat from his body at a very fast pace. Just as Pierre had convinced himself that he would be stuck in the mud for days, a group of teenagers came along. They had an old straw mattress that they had lit on fire to keep warm. They tossed it into the gutter, and it landed right on top of Pierre. By the time he was able to gather enough energy to stand up, the flames were inches away from his face.

"It's the ghost of the gutter!" one of the boys yelled. Pierre screamed and ran in one direction. The boys ran in another.

"What are you running from?" Pierre asked himself when he had calmed down. "You silly man — those boys were as afraid of you as you were of them."

Legs sore from running, Pierre tried to find his way back to the mattress, thinking that it would at least be warm. But not knowing which direction to walk, he turned again and again until he finally saw a light at the end of the street. As he glanced around, Pierre could see what looked like people of all shapes and sizes making their way down to the light.

Once his eyes adjusted, Pierre saw a man with no legs walking on his hands.

"Good charity, kind sir, and good night to you!" the man said as he moved past the poet. Another shape moved past Pierre. This time it was a man with one arm using a crutch. Pierre tried to move aside so the men could walk by with ease, but another one got in his way—a blind man with a long white beard. Each beggar held out his hand to Pierre to ask for a coin, but the poet had none to give. Pierre hung his head and started to walk away.

But the three misshapen men started walking behind him. If he sped up, they sped up. If he slowed down, they slowed down. Soon there was an entire parade of helpless men, lepers, and other beggars walking with him. Finally, after trying to turn back and make his way through the crowd, he came to a square.

"Where am I?" Pierre asked.

"Why, the Corner of Miracles," one of the beggars answered.

The Corner of Miracles was the place where thieves, gypsies, and other ruined members of Paris spent their nights. Fires blazed here and there in the wide-open square. Old, broken-down houses framed the area. Many strange people surrounded him, shouting, "Lead him to the king! To the king!"

"The k-k-k-ing?" Pierre stammered. "But doesn't he live in the palace?"

"Not that king, sonny, not that king!" an old man cried.

The crowd pushed him toward a run-down old tavern. Inside, worm-eaten tables surrounded the fireplace, which was red hot with a pot bubbling inside. Men and women who made their money on the streets surrounded poor Pierre.

The so-called king sat on top of a barrel beside the fire. His second in command, the legless man, said "Take off your hat." When Pierre didn't move, someone reached over and pulled it from his head.

"Well, well," the king said. "Who do we have here?"

The king was none other than the beggar who had ruined his play that morning, Clopin!

"What's your name?" Clopin asked him. "And what do you do? If you are not one of us, you'll be in quite a bit of trouble. This is our secret hide-away—no one but tramps, thieves, and beggars is allowed in here."

"My name is Pierre Gringoire. I am a poet."

"A poet? Well, that settles it. I told you only tramps, thieves, and beggars are allowed. Poets are most certainly not welcome here."

Pierre spun around and said, "Most powerful emperors and kings, surely you do not mean me any harm. I am a poet. I wrote the play many of you saw this morning. And look, I've nothing in my pockets. Many poets are tramps and thieves, just like you."

Clopin spoke quietly with the man beside him. "With all your soul," he asked Pierre, "do you join us as a tramp?"

Pierre nodded. "I do."

"Very well," said Clopin. "But first you must pass a test."

The tramps brought out a scarecrow and propped it up in the middle of the room.

"You must balance on one leg and pull the scarf from the scarecrow's pocket. If you can steal that scarf, you will prove that you are indeed a tramp and one of us."

"Fine," Pierre said, "although I might break my legs trying."

He stood up on a table
so he could reach the scarecrow's pocket, lifted up his
right foot, and swayed. The
scarecrow was very tall—at least
two feet taller than poor Pierre,
even when he was standing on the
table.

"Careful," Clopin said.
"The bells on his pockets
will chime if you miss!"

Pierre tried very hard to
stand still on one leg. The
table wobbled as he reached
his arm up above his head.
Just as he had the scarf in
his hands, he went tum-
bling onto the floor. The
scarf got caught in the
scarecrow's pocket, and the bells jingled loudly.

"Oh, no!" Pierre said.

"That's it," Clopin said, laughing. "You're done. Boys, round him up and get him out of here."

"Wait!"

The crowd parted, and the gypsy girl stood there. Cries of "Esmeralda!" rose up all around Pierre.

"Are you going to hurt this man?" she boldly asked Clopin.

"Why, yes, unless you ask us not to. You know that I look upon you as our queen, Esmeralda. If you think this man should be spared, then we'll do so, but I don't see why you'd want him to live."

"He tried to save me, when those awful men tried to take me away. So yes, I am asking that you spare him."

Pierre thought this must all be a dream, but then the men who were holding on to him let him go.

"You know that if you save him, you are responsible for him. We must settle it all with the jug."

"Fine." Esmeralda said. "Where is it?"

One of the tramps handed her the jug.

She gave it to Pierre. "Throw it on the floor."

He did exactly as she asked, and the jug broke into four pieces.

"There you have it," Clopin said. "By all of my power—you are now married for four years."

He pointed to Pierre. "You are free to go, but our laws say you must prove that you are one of us by the time those four years are up. Now get out of my sight."

# CHAPTER 5

## Not-So-Married Life

⌢

A few minutes later, Pierre found himself in a small, warm room. The girl moved quickly about and talked to Djali. She didn't notice him at all.

*What an angel,* Pierre thought. *She saved me.*

The poet stood up so quickly that Esmeralda was startled. "What do you want?" she asked.

Pierre was so overwhelmed by her beauty and kindness that he leaned in to kiss her. Esmeralda jumped away. "You are very rude!"

The goat moved between the two of them. Her painted horns looked very sharp to Pierre.

"Why did you rescue me, then?" he asked.

"I couldn't let them hurt you, could I? Not after you tried to save me from those awful men."

"That was your only reason?"

"My only reason."

"Well then, I promise I shall never try to kiss you again. Please, let's be friends. Can you ask the goat to move?"

Esmeralda looked at Pierre, and then at Djali. For a moment, she still looked angry, but then she laughed.

"Good, we can be as brother and sister," she said. "Now let's have some supper."

Esmeralda jumped down from the bed where she was standing. They sat quietly at the table and ate some bread and cheese. Esmeralda fed Djali some crumbs from her hands.

"Do you not believe in love, then?" Pierre asked her.

"Oh, yes, two people as one, it is heaven itself."

"But you do not love me?"

"You?" Esmeralda said, "No, for you have no helmet, no sword, and no horse."

"So if I had a horse you would love me?"

Esmeralda didn't answer him. She stared off into the distance. "The man I love must be able to protect me."

"Like from the hunchback, earlier this evening?" he said quietly.

Tears came quickly to her eyes. "That horrible hunchback."

Pierre wanted to talk some more. It was very rare for him to have any company, but he could tell Esmeralda wanted to be quiet for a bit.

"She's very pretty," Pierre said about Djali.

"Thank you. She's my only family."

"Why are you called Esmeralda?"

"I don't know. Maybe because of this—it's green, and *Esmeralda* means 'emerald.'" She pulled out a pendant to show him. It was a pouch made of green silk, with a large glass bead in the center. Pierre leaned forward and reached out his hand. "Oh, don't touch it," Esmeralda cried, "or else the spell might be broken."

"What spell?" Pierre asked. "Who gave it to you?" The girl didn't answer him. Instead, she tucked the necklace back into her clothes.

"Were you born in Paris?"

"No," Esmeralda answered. "I came here when I was a little girl." She looked at him. "I don't even know your name."

"I am Pierre. Pierre Gringoire."

The little encouragement was all Pierre needed. He happily told Esmeralda all about his family and about how he had come to Paris when he had turned sixteen. He told her that he had tried every kind of job before deciding to be a poet and a playwright, and that Archdeacon Claude Frollo had helped him learn his letters. "Why, I even know Latin," he said.

"If you know Latin, can you tell me what *Phœbus* means?" Esmeralda asked.

Pierre was confused about what that had to do with his speech, but he answered her anyway. "It means 'the sun.'"

"The sun?" she said.

"Yes, it is the name of a handsome archer who was a god."

"A god!" Esmeralda said. Just then, one of her golden bracelets fell to the ground, and Pierre bent over to pick it up. As he sat back up, he heard the bolt on the door click. Esmeralda had gone into another room.

"Well, then," Pierre said as he stood up and walked around the small room. "I might as well go to sleep." He found a long chest that would work as a bed and lay down. He had barely rested his head on the hard wood before he was fast asleep.

CHAPTER 6

# The Priest and the Hunchback

‿◌

Archdeacon Claude Frollo came from a noble family. He had wanted to become a priest ever since he was a small boy. As a child, he had learned Latin. He read all the time and took his studies very seriously.

Sadly, his parents had died in the great plague of 1466. Claude became the head of the family and took care of his baby brother, Jehan. It was hard to do both—study and take care of his brother—but Claude Frollo managed. By the time Jehan was twenty, Claude Frollo had become a priest at Notre-Dame.

Despite Claude Frollo's guidance, Jehan had grown wild, like a tree. The more Jehan fooled around, the more seriously Claude Frollo studied. The more he read, the more interested he became in alchemy and astrology.

A rumor soon began to spread that Claude Frollo had built a secret room in the church. Hidden behind closed doors, they said, he practiced magic.

One day, Claude Frollo was called over by two old women standing near the church's pews. The two widows had found a small child in a wooden bed by the statue of Saint Christopher. He was wrapped in a burlap sack, his head poking out from the top. He had a forest of red hair, crooked teeth, and one eye.

When Claude Frollo heard the cries of the

poor child, he knew he had to take care of him, just as he had taken care of little Jehan.

So Claude Frollo said to the widows, "I shall adopt this poor child."

Frollo picked up the child and wrapped him in his own robes as he walked away.

He baptized the boy and called him Quasimodo. The two were happy together.

By the time the boy was fourteen, Claude Frollo had gotten Quasimodo the job of bell ringer at Notre-Dame, and the church became his whole world. As a child, he could often be found climbing around the stones and pulling himself up and down the stairs. Quasimodo took to the cathedral like a snail does to his shell. Inside the walls of the church, no one teased him or called him names. Inside he felt safe.

No one in Paris knew the ins and outs of Notre-Dame like Quasimodo. There was no corner he hadn't explored, no tower he hadn't climbed — sometimes from the outside! — and no marble stone he hadn't touched.

The windows gave him all the light he needed. The statues were his friends, the stone birds, his pets. But what made him the happiest? Why, the bells, of course. He talked to them in his own language. He loved how they felt and the sounds they made. There were fifteen bells that Quasimodo rang, different chimes for different days. On days like Christmas, he rang all of them!

Quasimodo had only one real friend in the world — Claude Frollo, who had taught him to read, to write, and to speak. Even when Claude Frollo was harsh with him and spoke in an angry voice, Quasimodo loved him. When Quasimodo had gone deaf from the ringing of the bells, he and Claude Frollo had created their own sign language. Quasimodo would do anything Claude Frollo told him to — no questions asked. Even if it meant kidnapping a girl.

## CHAPTER 7

# Sir Robert and the Day's Trials

～∽

Sir Robert, the mayor of Paris, was usually a very happy man. But on the morning of January 7, 1482, he woke up in a foul temper.

Where did this bad mood come from? He knew the city was a mess from the festival, and he had to make sure it got cleaned up. He would also have to spend a day in court listening to all the problems from the day before, and festivals *always* created a lot of problems. By all accounts, it was going to be a very long day!

And now Sir Robert was running late. The trials had begun at eight o'clock that morning. Dozens of people were crowded into the small room of the main courthouse. Two sergeants, in their bright red-and-blue jackets, stood by the door. A clerk sat nearby, writing quickly. The judge was old and deaf, which always presented a number of problems.

Many of the same students who had attended the play were in the audience watching the cases. One of them was Jehan, Claude Frollo's brother. He was there with his friend Joannes. The two laughed and joked about the people the judge punished.

"Joannes." Jehan tapped his friend on the shoulder to grab his attention. "It's Quasimodo, our Pope of Fools, the one-eyed hunchback that my brother pities."

Sure enough, there was Quasimodo with his

hands and feet tied up. An entire company of soldiers stood around him, but he didn't make a sound. The clerk handed the judge the charges against Quasimodo. The judge went to great lengths to conceal his deafness. He always read the files beforehand so he wouldn't have too many questions. Now he threw back his head and shut his eyes. The room fell quiet.

"What's your name?" the judge shouted.

Quasimodo, who was of course also deaf, did not answer. The judge carried on. "Fine. Your age?" Again the hunchback said nothing.

"Well then, you are accused of mischief, of making a nighttime disturbance, of attacking a girl, and of refusing arrest. What do you have to say for yourself?"

A roar of laughter took over the room. Even the clerk was giggling. Quasimodo turned around and shrugged. The judge thought that Quasimodo had made them laugh.

"Do you realize how much trouble you are in?" he asked. "Do you know to whom you are speaking?"

The last question made everyone laugh even harder. Quasimodo had still not said a word. Now the hunchback and the judge were the only two people in the room not giggling. Even the soldiers on guard shook with laughter.

The judge wanted Quasimodo to fear him, so he shouted, "How dare you act this way in front of a judge! *I* am in charge here—*I* make the rules—"

Suddenly the door opened and Sir Robert appeared. "Mister Mayor," the judge shouted, "I demand to know how you are going to punish this man!"

The mayor worked his way through the crowd and sat down in his chair. Then he turned to Quasimodo and said, "What have you done to end up here?"

But Quasimodo thought Sir Robert was asking his name. "Quasimodo," he replied in his harsh, raspy voice.

Sir Robert became angry. "Are you making fun of me?"

Now Quasimodo thought Sir Robert was asking what he did for a living. "Bell ringer at Notre-Dame," he answered.

The giggling started up again. "Bell ringer?" the mayor asked. His mood had not improved. "What are you talking about?"

"I will be twenty in a few months, I think," Quasimodo said.

Quasimodo's strange answers made the mayor lose his temper. "Take him outside and throw some cold water on him—that should scare him into making sense."

But the judge had finally figured out what was going on. "Goodness me, he's deaf! He doesn't need to have water thrown at him. Let's just put him in the stocks at the Place de Grève for an hour. With his head and hands bound in the wooden slates, he should learn his lesson."

"Well done!" Joannes and Jehan shouted. "Well done."

⌒∽

The Place de Grève was a mess! Rags, ribbons, feathers, and drops of wax covered the square. The shopkeepers were all outside greeting anyone who passed.

Members of the King's Guard had been standing watch beside the stocks all morning. People knew this meant someone was going to be punished that day—so they waited.

Soon shouts were heard as the guards brought Quasimodo forward. It was quite a sight—the Pope of Fools, now a lowly prisoner. Yet Quasimodo remained calm. He didn't cry or shout.

"Look at him!" Jehan said to Joannes. "He has no idea what is going to happen to him."

A scary-looking man led Quasimodo to the stocks. When he realized that the giant wooden blocks were to be his prison, Quasimodo began to shake. The look on his face made everyone laugh, for he was terrified. The man pulled Quasimodo's arms toward the stocks and forced his head into place. At first, the hunchback fought and shook the stocks for all he was worth, but then they were locked in place. Quasimodo's face fell. He closed his one eye and let his head drop as far as the wooden prison would allow.

CHAPTER 8

# The Rat Hole

❦

The building to the west of the square had once been owned by a lovely young woman who had become very sad after her father died in a war. She mourned him by closing up the house and living in a tiny room on the first floor. When she died, she left her house behind for the sole purpose of being a place of mourning. The small room, closed up and dark except for a window with bars but no glass, was known around the square as the Rat Hole. An old hag called the Sack Woman lived inside.

On the day Quasimodo went to the stocks, two women were walking toward the Rat Hole. One of them, Anne, was the mayor's wife. The second, Sophie, was her cousin from the country. Sophie held her son's hand. His name was Eustache, and he was carrying a cake for the old woman.

"Come on, Sophie," Anne said. "We don't want to be late. My husband said the hunchback would only be in the stocks for an hour. That doesn't leave us much time to do our good deed and give the cake to the Sack Woman."

On their way, the two ladies gossiped about the events of the day before. "Wait!" Sophie said suddenly. "What's that?"

In the distance, the women could hear a tambourine. "It must be the gypsy, Esmeralda, playing and dancing with her goat," Anne answered. "Quick, let's go see. I bet little Eustache would like it very much!"

"A gypsy!" Sophie stopped in her tracks. "No, she might steal my boy. Come, Eustache."

Sophie pulled her son along behind her as she ran toward the Place de Grève. Finally, when she could no longer run, she stopped. Soon Anne caught up to her. "Goodness, what is the matter? What do you mean the gypsy will steal your boy?"

Sophie just shook her head.

"You know," Anne said, "come to think of it, the old Sack Woman in the Rat Hole thinks the same thing of the gypsies."

"Really?" Sophie asked.

"Why, yes," Anne answered. "I heard about it just the other day."

"You see, I would not wish the fate of Paquette on anyone," Sophie said.

"Who is that?" Anne asked. "I have never heard of Paquette. You *must* tell me the story!"

"Paquette was a young woman from Reims who suffered a terrible tragedy when she was just eighteen. Her father died when she was small, and even though she came from a good family, she and her mother were very poor. A few years after her mother's death, Paquette gave birth to a baby girl.

"The baby's name was Agnes, and Paquette placed all of her hopes and dreams upon her. The girl was even more beautiful than Paquette. Then one day the gypsies came to Reims. They had come to tell fortunes, but they were banned from the city, so they camped on its outskirts. Of course, the entire town went to see them. Paquette wanted to know what would happen to her daughter, so she carried her off to see the gypsies.

"The fortune-tellers said she'd be a queen and a great beauty. Paquette was overjoyed. The next day, she left Agnes asleep for just a moment while she went to tell a neighbor the good news. When she returned home, she was surprised not to hear the baby crying.

"*Maybe she's still asleep,* Paquette thought, but

when she opened the door to the room, Agnes was gone! Paquette rushed downstairs, crying, 'Someone has stolen my child!'

"The only thing left behind was a tiny satin shoe.

"The street was empty, and no one she asked had seen the girl. As Paquette returned to her room, she heard a baby's cry. *Why, it must be Agnes!* she thought.

"But it wasn't. She opened the door to find a one-eyed, deformed, limping baby—a little monster who looked about four years old.

"Paquette screamed and ran back outside. 'The gypsies have stolen my baby and replaced her with a monster!' she cried out.

"Everyone in Reims went out to find Agnes, but the gypsies were gone. About two miles out of town, they found one of the girl's ribbons. The very next day, Paquette's hair turned gray. The day after that, she disappeared."

Sophie finished her tale and looked at her cousin. Anne was very pale. "I can see why you are afraid of gypsies," she said.

"No one knows what happened to Paquette," Sophie said. "Some say she drowned in the river. Others say she walked to Paris barefoot."

"What happened to the gypsy monster?" Anne asked. "Did he drown with Paquette?"

"No, not at all," Sophie said. "Someone left him at Notre-Dame. Our archdeacon felt sorry for him, blessed him, and let him live there."

The trio had arrived at the Place de Grève. Caught up in all the excitement of Paquette's story, they had forgotten who was in the stocks. When they realized it was Quasimodo, they stopped dead. He was the gypsy monster from the story! If it hadn't been for Eustache tugging on his mother's arm, asking if he could eat the cake, they would have stood there frozen in shock.

"Oh, we almost forgot about the Rat Hole," Sophie said quietly. "Come, let's go now and bring the poor woman the cake. We don't need to watch this!"

Anne and Sophie walked over to the other side of the square and stood in front of the window of the Rat Hole. They stood on their toes and looked inside. The dark room held a skinny woman with gray hair. She was curled up with her hands around her knees. It was very cold in the room, and she had no winter clothes.

"We shouldn't bother her," Sophie said.

"You know, I can imagine Paquette in a place like this—punishing herself because of what happened to her beautiful girl," Anne said.

Just then, Sophie saw a child's shoe in the room. She gasped. "Look! It's the shoe, the tiny satin shoe! It *is* Paquette!"

Anne cried out.

Eustache said, "Mother, please, can I eat that cake?"

The boy's voice woke the Sack Woman from her trance. "Is that a child I hear? Take him away! Take him away before the gypsies come!" She crawled on her knees toward the shoe, then sighed and collapsed.

A commotion broke out around the stocks, and it roused the Sack Woman. She rushed to the window and shouted, "Aha! It must be the gypsy who calls me!"

She stretched both of her thin arms between the bars and shouted, "So it is you, gypsy woman! You child stealer, curse you! A curse upon all of you!"

Sophie screamed, and she and Anne ran away, pulling Eustache behind them.

CHAPTER 9

# Quasimodo in the Stocks

♾

The crowd around the stocks laughed and threw rocks at Quasimodo. He was an easy target, and crowds often threw all kinds of things at prisoners in the stocks.

Quasimodo shook the stocks and rocked back and forth. His face turned red. Then he saw Claude Frollo on his horse—he thought he was saved! But the priest did not stay. He kicked his heels, and the horse took off.

"Water!" Quasimodo shouted in his raspy voice.

The people around the stocks laughed even harder. The more Quasimodo moved around, the thirstier he became. "Water!"

Joannes threw a dirty sponge from the gutter at Quasimodo. "There's water for you."

"Water!" Quasimodo roared.

At that very moment, Esmeralda walked through the crowd with Djali. She saw that Quasimodo was in trouble and went right up to him. She pulled out a bottle full of water and gave it to him to drink.

Esmeralda could never stand to see people in pain. She knew Quasimodo had suffered enough, and she had a feeling it hadn't been his idea to try to kidnap her. She had seen the man in the cape race away from the square. It made her shudder to think about him.

The people in the crowd were touched by Esmeralda's kindness. They stopped laughing and teasing the hunchback.

When the Sack Woman spied Esmeralda from her window, she shouted, "Cursed gypsy girl! A curse upon you!"

Esmeralda turned pale. She quickly stepped down from the stocks and ran away as fast as she could. By now, Quasimodo's punishment had ended. He was set free, and the crowd slowly moved away.

As he walked back to Notre-Dame, Quasimodo hung his head in shame, a very sad man indeed. Why had Claude Frollo not helped him? What had he done wrong?

*His eyes looked so cold,* Quasimodo thought, *and I never would have been in those stocks if I hadn't been doing what he wanted me to.*

In fact, if not for the very same gypsy girl that Claude Frollo had wanted them to take the night before, Quasimodo would have had a far worse time in the stocks than he did. But still, he didn't understand Claude Frollo's behavior.

# CHAPTER 10

# Esmeralda Meets Captain Phœbus Again

⁓

The sun was shining and people were out and about, enjoying springtime in Paris. In Dame Aloise's beautiful apartment just across from Notre-Dame, a group of lovely young noblewomen were laughing. Fleur-de-Lis, Dame Aloise's daughter, was giggling with her friends.

Dame Aloise sat in a plush velvet chair with a tall young man by her side. It was Captain Phœbus, who had saved Esmeralda all those months ago.

Every now and again, Dame Aloise would

speak to Captain Phœbus. Then she would look over at her daughter and say something like, "Look how well she does with her needlework."

"Yes, indeed," the captain would reply.

"Did you ever see such a pretty girl as your fiancée?" Dame Aloise asked the captain. "She's as beautiful as a swan, isn't she?"

"Yes, indeed," he replied again, even though he wasn't thinking of Fleur-de-Lis.

"Oh, go and speak with her!" Dame Aloise pushed him toward Fleur-de-Lis. "You've been far too quiet today."

Phœbus walked over and said, "What is the subject of your tapestry, Fleur-de-Lis?"

"The lovely caves in Italy known as Neptune's Grotto," she answered. "That makes the third time you've asked."

"Oh," he said.

Phœbus knew he was supposed to bend over

and whisper words of love into her ear, but he couldn't think of anything more to say.

"Is 'oh' all you have to say to me?" Fleur-de-Lis raised her pretty blue eyes to him.

Phœbus did not quite know what to do next, so he stood up and almost shouted, "What a charming tapestry!"

All at once, the girls started talking about tapestries, each trying to get Captain Phœbus to speak to her. One of them looked up and out of the window and said, "There's a girl dancing and playing the tambourine in the square."

"Some gypsy, I daresay," Fleur-de-Lis said, turning back to her sewing.

"Oh, let's see, let's see!" The other girls scrambled up and to the window. Phœbus was relieved when they moved away from him. He knew Dame Aloise wanted him to marry her daughter, but he had other girls on his mind.

"Captain Phœbus," Fleur-de-Lis said, "did

you not tell us a grand story about how you res-
cued a gypsy girl? Maybe it's the girl outside?"

Phœbus walked over to the balcony where all
the girls were watching. With the windows open,
the girls could hear the bells of Notre-Dame ringing in the distance.

"Why yes, that is her goat."

"Look at that man on the roof of the church!"
one of the girls said.

"It's the archdeacon, Claude Frollo—look
how he stares!" another said. "How strange that
he should be so interested in a gypsy girl."

"Captain," Fleur-de-Lis said, "call down to the
gypsy girl and tell her to come up to us. It would
be such fun."

"I doubt she would remember me," he said.

Fleur-de-Lis looked at him and pouted.

"All right, then," he said. "I'll do it."

"Little girl!" he called from the balcony.

Esmeralda stopped and looked up at him. "Over here!"

Esmeralda blushed. She started walking through the circle of people toward the house.

Moments later, she was upstairs in the apartment. The girls were dazzled by her beauty. This made them very quiet and unhappy.

Phœbus broke the silence. "What a charming girl! Don't you think so, Fleur-de-Lis?"

"Not bad," she said, and the other girls started to whisper.

"Do you remember me?" Phœbus asked Esmeralda.

"Oh, yes, I do," she said sweetly.

He smiled and said, "You slipped away that night we met and left that hunchback in your place. Did I frighten you?"

"Oh, no," Esmeralda answered. Fleur-de-Lis did not like this conversation between Phœbus and the gypsy girl. In fact, she did not like Phœbus to speak to *any* other girl.

"What did that monster of a fellow want with you?" he asked.

"I don't know," the gypsy girl replied.

"Well, he was punished for what he did. You know he spent time in the stocks," the captain told her.

"Yes, I know. They were very cruel to him that day. The poor fellow!" Esmeralda said.

"Goodness me!" Dame Aloise shouted. "What's this beast?" Djali had gotten herself tangled up in the folds of the old woman's skirt.

"It's a goat!" Fleur-de-Lis said. "I've heard of this goat—make it do a trick."

"I don't know what you mean," Esmeralda said.

"Come on," one of the girls said. "What's that around your neck?"

Esmeralda held the tiny bag in her hands. "Why, that's my secret."

Dame Aloise was growing tired of the girl. "If you aren't going to dance for us, why did you come upstairs? Leave now. You don't belong here."

Esmeralda started to cry as she made her way to the door. She took one look back at Phœbus, who said, "You can't leave like this. Come back and give us a dance! Besides, you haven't even told us your name."

"Esmeralda," she said as she untied a rope from the goat's neck and opened up the pouch. The letters of the alphabet spilled out on to the floor. Djali started to shuffle them together with her pretty little foot.

"Look, look at what the goat has done!" one of the girls called out.

Fleur-de-Lis stormed over and saw that Djali had spelled out PHŒBUS. "The goat did this?" she asked.

"Yes, she did," her friend answered.

*69*

"How did it know to do that? You must be a witch!" Fleur-de-Lis said angrily to Esmeralda. And then she fainted. The girls rushed toward her.

Esmeralda quickly picked up her letters and left the apartment. Phœbus looked at the girls clustered around Fleur-de-Lis and made up his mind. He left the apartment and followed the gypsy.

⌒

Claude Frollo had been sitting on top of Notre-Dame's tower, watching Esmeralda.

*Who is that man with her?* he wondered as he saw a figure push the crowd back. *Why, it's Pierre Gringoire, but what would he be doing with her?*

Claude Frollo went outside to find out what was going on, but by then Esmeralda had disappeared.

"Where did the girl go?" Claude Frollo demanded of the man standing next to him.

"I don't know. She just left and went up into that building. Someone called to her from the window."

Claude Frollo walked over to Esmeralda's small carpet, where she usually stood and danced. "What are you doing here?" he asked Pierre.

The stern voice of the Claude Frollo scared the poet. He stammered a hello.

"Are you no longer a poet, but a street performer?" Claude Frollo asked.

Pierre explained that his play at the Great Hall had been a disaster and that he was now with the tramps of the Corner of Miracles.

"How do you know the gypsy girl?" Claude Frollo asked.

"She is my wife and I am her husband," Pierre answered.

Claude Frollo became very angry, "What do you mean? You are not married to Esmeralda?"

Pierre started to shake. "Oh, it's not what you think." He told the archdeacon how Esmeralda had saved him from certain death.

Claude Frollo asked Pierre all about Esmeralda, and the poet told him everything he knew. "Oh, and it took her two months to teach Djali to spell *Phœbus,*" Pierre added.

"Why *Phœbus*?" Claude Frollo asked.

"She thinks it's a magical word," Pierre answered.

"Is it a word or a name?" Claude Frollo asked.

"Why do you care, sir," the poet asked.

Claude Frollo grew angry and shouted for Pierre to leave. The fact of the matter was that he was in love with Esmeralda. He had seen her playing her tambourine and dancing, and knew that she had to be his—no matter what.

# CHAPTER 11

# Jehan's Adventures

c⌒ɔ

The next morning, as Jehan Frollo was getting dressed for the day, he noticed that his purse was empty—he had no money.

"Oh, how cruel," he said to the empty bit of fabric. "You have been completely emptied by my nightly fun."

Jehan pulled on his shoes and told himself that he would have to go see his brother. *He'll give me a lecture,* he thought, *but at least I'll get some money.*

On his way to the church, Jehan smelled the tasty bread in the bakeries. But he had no money for breakfast. When he finally arrived at Notre-Dame, he couldn't decide whether or not to go inside. He paced about for a few minutes, thinking.

*I do not want to sit through a great speech this morning,* he thought as he stepped back and forth in front of the main steps. *But I do need those coins.*

"Have you seen the archdeacon?" he asked a man coming down the church's front steps.

"I believe he's locked himself in his tower," the fellow said as he walked away.

Jehan took off his cap and walked inside. *At last! I'll get to see that room where my brother locks himself away.*

Jehan was out of breath by the time he made his way to the room at the top of the steps. The key was in the door, and Jehan pushed it open. The room was dark. A great armchair and a table sat in the middle of it, surrounded by compasses, animal skeletons, a giant globe, and glass jars filled with all kinds of liquids. Books lay open all over the floor, and there were cobwebs in all the corners.

A large fireplace stood in one corner, Jehan noticed, but it hadn't been lit. A pair of dusty bellows sat beside it. The walls had writing in all

kinds of languages on them. The entire room seemed to be falling apart.

Claude Frollo was sitting in the armchair, leaning over a large book filled with pictures. His back was to the door, and he didn't hear it open. He was also talking to himself. Jehan didn't want to interrupt, but he did want his money.

*My brother is crazy,* he thought. Then, realizing that he had seen things he probably wasn't meant to see, Jehan stepped back, closed the door quietly, and knocked loudly.

"Come in, Sir Robert!" Claude Frollo said. "I have been waiting for you."

Jehan pushed open the door and boldly entered the room.

"Jehan!" the archdeacon cried. "Is it you?"

"Yes." He tried to smile.

Claude Frollo looked angry for a moment, and then said, "What are you doing here?"

"I came . . ." Jehan began. "I came to ask for some coins." Claude Frollo's face turned red. "And some good advice, for I am in need of both," Jehan added.

"I have heard talk of your bad behavior all over Paris," Claude Frollo said. "Why do you need the coins?"

"For charity," Jehan answered.

"We give enough to charity here, from the church. What more noble causes could you be giving money to?"

"Umm," Jehan started, "to the Sack Woman who lives in the Rat Hole."

"And how are your studies? Aristotle? Horace?" Claude Frollo asked, changing the subject.

"My books are lost and stolen."

"Jehan, I am very upset with you."

"So not even a few coins to buy some bread?"

"He who does not work, does not eat."

Jehan leaned over and sobbed. Then he stuck one hand up into the air and recited a long, detailed speech in Greek.

"Now, what is that?" Claude Frollo asked.

"It's Æschylus—it's about expressing one's grief over life."

Claude Frollo laughed. "That was very good, but I'm still not giving you any coins."

"Not even for new shoes? See how my soles stick out like tongues?"

"I'll send you new shoes, but no money." Suddenly Claude Frollo heard someone coming up the stairs. "Jehan, you need to hide. That will be Sir Robert. He cannot know you are here."

"Aha! I'll hide, but only for the coins."

"Fine, fine, just get into the closet!" Claude Frollo said as he handed his brother the money.

Jehan hid, but he could still see and hear what was going on. After saying good day to each other,

Sir Robert and Claude Frollo spoke quietly for a moment.

Finally the mayor said, "Shall I instruct the guard to arrest the gypsy witch for casting spells so that you can bring her here to the church?"

"No — not yet," Claude Frollo said. "I will tell you when."

In the meantime, Jehan had found a hard crust of bread in the closet. Sir Robert heard a loud crunch and said, "What on earth was that?"

Claude Frollo looked over at the closet and replied, "Oh, it must be my cat. She has probably found a mouse." He got up from his chair. "Why don't we take a walk around Notre-Dame, explore the walls again?"

The two of them left the room, which made Jehan quite happy, as his legs had fallen asleep by this point. "Ouch! Oh! Ouch!" he cried as he crawled out of the closet.

He shook his purse and was very pleased to hear it rattle. He dusted himself off and took one more look around the room. It certainly was a strange place.

On his way out, Jehan saw his brother and the mayor examining one of the sculptures on the side of the church, talking about signs and history.

"What is that to me? I've got my coins! Ah, fresh air of Paris!" Jehan took a deep breath and stamped his feet, "Oh, good sidewalk! I am glad to be standing here instead of crouching in that closet."

Suddenly, Jehan heard someone shouting from behind him.

"That sounds just like Captain Phœbus," he said. Jehan turned to see the captain standing there.

The archdeacon had heard his brother say Phœbus's name and looked over to see Jehan shake the tall officer's hand.

That was the name Pierre had said to him! *This is the man Esmeralda loves. He is my sworn enemy!* Claude Frollo thought.

"Phœbus!" Jehan cried. "Why are you yelling?"

"Oh, I have just spent another morning with Fleur-de-Lis and her friends. It always makes me yell."

"Come on," Jehan said, "Let's go to the Rose and Crown for lunch."

"But I don't have any money."

Jehan tapped his purse. "I have!"

"Where did you get all that?" Phœbus asked as Jehan jingled the purse between them.

"Ah, from my brother, the idiot archdeacon."

"Well, then." Phœbus smiled. "Let's go spend that money!"

The archdeacon made his excuses to Sir Robert and followed Phœbus and his brother.

In the distance, the men heard the faint sound of a tambourine.

"Blood and thunder!" Phœbus shouted. "Let's go faster."

"Why?" Jehan asked.

"I don't want to see that gypsy girl."

"The one with the goat?"

"The very same. I've convinced her to meet me tonight and I don't want to see her before then." Phœbus winked at Jehan and broke out into a wide grin. "I've almost got her convinced that I actually do love her. If she sees me now, she'll think I'm following her. Then I will never be able to get rid of her."

"You are a lucky fellow," Jehan said and patted his friend on the shoulder. "A lucky fellow indeed."

A shudder ran straight through Claude Frollo's spine — the last thing he wanted was the man Esmeralda loved getting any closer to her!

# CHAPTER 12

# The Man in the Black Cape

⁓

The Rose and Crown was a very busy place. Claude Frollo paced for hours, waiting for Jehan and Phœbus to leave. When he finally saw his brother and the captain emerge, he followed them down the road.

"Do you have any money left, Jehan?" Phœbus asked.

Jehan didn't answer. Instead he started singing.

"There's nothing left in my pouch," Jehan said finally, "which is my cue to go home." Jehan tipped his hat to Phœbus and made his way down the street.

Phœbus stopped in front of a statue to catch his breath. When he heard steps behind him, he spun around.

"Who's there?" Phœbus called out. "You've nothing to rob from me."

"Captain Phœbus!" Claude Frollo shouted from under the black cape he was wearing.

"How do you know my name?" Phœbus asked.

"Not only do I know your name, but I know where you are going as well."

"You do not—show your face! Let's fight it out." Phœbus put his fists up in the air.

"You are planning to meet the gypsy girl."

"How did you know that?" Phœbus swung at the strange man but didn't hit him.

"You will *not* go to her. If you do, I will surely hurt you, for you do not deserve her."

"What are you talking about, you crazy old man? I am going to meet the girl whether you like it or not," Phœbus said angrily as he drew his sword. "I will fight you right here and now if you don't let me pass."

"There's no need for swords," Claude Frollo said. "I know you have no money. I am coming with you, and I will pay you to let me speak to her."

"What—" Phœbus began. "Wait, you'll pay me? Very well, you can come along, but this is all very strange."

Phœbus led them to a small, dingy inn run by an old hag. The walls were cracked and falling apart. "You go in first," Phœbus said. "And hide. I'll be back with the girl soon. You can talk to her for a moment, but that's it. After that, you'll have to leave."

Claude Frollo stepped into the room and took off his hood. He waited as his eyes adjusted to the darkness. Suddenly he heard the stairs creak. Seeing a light under the doorway, he quickly hid inside a closet.

The old woman let Phœbus and Esmeralda into the room. At first, Claude Frollo could hardly believe she was there. She was so beautiful, he almost fainted from the sight of her. Even though it was wrong, he had never loved anything — not his brother, not his books, not the church — the way he loved Esmeralda.

Esmeralda was upset. She did not like meeting Phœbus alone in an inn. But he told her again and again that he loved her.

"I do not think that I should be here." Esmeralda said to him. "I am breaking a promise, and I will never find my parents now. My charm will lose its power. I promised my gypsy family when they gave me the pouch that I would be good, and being alone with you is not good."

"I wish I understood what you were talking about," Phœbus said.

Esmeralda stood there quietly with Djali at her feet. "I do love you, Captain Phœbus."

"You do?" he asked and put an arm around her waist.

"You are kind and saved me from the man in the black cape that night." She moved away from his arm. "I can never thank you enough."

He stepped closer to her, but Esmeralda moved again. Every time Phœbus took a step closer to her, she moved away.

"Do you love me?" she asked.

He sank to one knee. "As I have never loved another."

"I am so happy I could die," Esmeralda said.

"Why should you want to die? You are beautiful." Phœbus stepped in closer and tried to give her a kiss.

But Esmeralda ducked and stood next to the window. She had vowed never to kiss a man until she was either married or reunited with her parents.

"If you love me as you say you do, then we can be married."

"Who needs marriage? We can be happy here, together, forever. I'm yours and you're mine. We don't need a church and a ceremony to tell us that! What use is marriage to two people who love each other as we do?" Phœbus stepped forward again and stood very close to Esmeralda.

The entire scene made Claude Frollo's veins run cold. The silly captain was trying to take advantage of Esmeralda, trying to make her believe he loved her so that he could kiss her! But Claude Frollo knew he did not truly love her. She was so good, so honest. And the captain's intentions were anything but good.

*The rascal,* Claude Frollo thought, *the weasel. Oh, I'll teach him!*

Phœbus grabbed Esmeralda's shawl and pulled it off her shoulders. He could clearly see the pouch around her neck. "What is that?" he asked. "I saw it yesterday when you were at the apartment."

"Please, Captain Phœbus. It's my charm. It will help me find my parents. Please give me back my shawl."

"You do not love me," Phœbus pouted.

"But I do, I do. Even if we can't be married, I want to be with you all the time. I don't need anything but air and love. Oh, what does it matter anymore. Maybe I'll never find my parents anyway. They've stayed away from me for this long."

Esmeralda stepped toward him, prepared to kiss him, and Claude Frollo crashed through the closet door. Before Esmeralda knew what was happening, she fainted.

# CHAPTER 13

## Poor Esmeralda

Pierre didn't know what to do. Esmeralda had been missing for over a month. One day, as he was out looking for her, he passed the prison, where a crowd of people had gathered.

"What's going on?" he asked a young student.

"I don't know, sir. I think they are trying a girl for almost killing a soldier. I tried to talk to my brother, the archdeacon, about it, but I couldn't get anywhere near him. I was hoping to ask him for some money."

Pierre realized that he must be speaking to Jehan. "I am sorry, young sir, but I have none to give, either."

Jehan shrugged and wandered off down the street. Pierre followed the crowd up the stairs and into the courthouse.

"Who are all these people?" Pierre asked as he looked around. "And who is the accused?"

"Well," said the old man standing next to him, "the woman with her back to us, there"—he pointed—"is the one who is charged with attempted murder. And there's an old hag on the stand as we speak. She's a witness."

The old woman he pointed to was saying, "I know this girl did not harm that officer. I saw her that night. Before she came in, I let a strange cloaked man into the room. I heard a scream and ran upstairs just in time to see a dark figure jump out of the window and into the river. He left behind him the poor captain, who lay nearly dead on the floor."

The crowd murmured, and Sir Robert said, "Just before he disappeared, Captain Phœbus told us that he did not remember what had happened to the caped man. All he could say was that this man wanted to meet the gypsy girl. He offered to pay for the room if he could hide in the closet."

At last, the accused turned around. Pierre was shocked to see that it was Esmeralda! She looked terrible. Her lips were blue from the cold, and her hair was messy.

"Bring in the second prisoner!" Sir Robert said.

A door opened and Djali was led into the room. The lawyers stood in front of the poor creature and made her perform her tricks. Pierre could not hold his tongue anymore. "Can't you see that Djali doesn't know she is doing anything wrong! She's just a goat!"

But the crowd ignored him. Then Sir Robert spilled Djali's bag of letters onto the floor. Djali moved them, one by one, into the name PHŒBUS.

Finally Sir Robert said, "Gypsy girl, you are responsible for the harm that came to Captain Phœbus. You and your goat bewitched him and then left him for dead. Do you dare to deny this?"

"Oh, my poor Phœbus. This is too awful for words," Esmeralda cried.

"I repeat, gypsy girl, do you deny these charges?" Sir Robert asked again.

"I told you. I don't know what happened. There is a man—a stranger to me—who follows me. He even tried to kidnap me once. Captain Phœbus saved me. Why would I hurt him?"

Sir Robert looked at her sternly and said, "You were the only one in the room when we found the soldier. And your goat can spell his name. Tomorrow you will be put into the stocks until you tell us the truth. You will be there without food or water until you confess."

Esmeralda did not say a word. Pierre could not believe his ears. The lawyers, the mayor, and the judge followed as the guards led the girl to her cell.

The jail was cold, damp, and dark. No windows graced the walls. Esmeralda tried to be brave, but she was scared.

"For the last time," Sir Robert said, "do you deny that the attack on Captain Phœbus was your doing?"

Esmeralda could not speak. She merely nodded.

The guards pushed her inside the cell. "Very well. You will remain here until the morning. Then you will be put into the stocks."

With every last ounce of energy she had, Esmeralda declared, "I am innocent!"

The door closed behind her, leaving Esmeralda in total darkness. She heard rats scratching at the walls and a faint *drip, drip, drip* behind her. Djali was not with her, and the world felt so small, the floor so cold, the walls so wet. She remembered how awful the stocks had been for poor Quasimodo. How the people had made fun of him and thrown things at him. Esmeralda couldn't bear the thought that everyone would see her.

"Wait!" Esmeralda called. "Wait! I confess. It's all my fault. I confess!"

The door opened and Sir Robert stood there. "You confess to it all?"

"Yes, yes, I do."

"Good girl," Sir Robert said.

Esmeralda was led back into the courtroom. Djali bleated and would have run to her, but she was tied to the bench.

"The girl has confessed to everything," Sir Robert said.

"Punish me quickly," Esmeralda said. "That is all I ask."

The mayor made a very long speech and then came her punishment—both she and Djali were to be sent to the prison under Notre-Dame—forever!

⌒

The prison at Notre-Dame grew darker and gloomier the farther down it went. Once the prisoners were sent down there, it was unlikely that they would ever be released. The guards took Esmeralda down to her cell. Weighed down by chains, she was but a ghost of her dancing self.

She had been there for a few days when the door to her cell opened and someone stepped inside. The light blinded her, and she closed her eyes. When she opened them, Claude Frollo stood there wearing his dark cloak.

"Who are you?" she asked. "What are you doing here?"

"Come with me." He pulled down his hood.

"Where . . . where do you want to take me?"

The priest did not answer.

"It's you! You were there that night. It was you who hurt Phœbus, wasn't it?" Esmeralda asked. "Why did you try to kidnap me? Why do you hate me?"

"Hate you? I love you," he said. "I was happy before I knew you."

"Alas," she said, "so was I."

"Please, let me speak." Claude Frollo told the gypsy girl how he had come to love her. How he had seen her, day after day in the square by Notre-Dame. Even though he knew it was wrong, he loved her. Her dancing, her dress, her pretty skin—all of these things took him away from his studies, away from what he had known his entire life.

"A spirit I could not control took hold of me," he said. "I could not forget you. And that day, that awful day, I followed him. I hid in the closet, and just when you were about to kiss that rogue, I jumped out and attacked him."

"Oh, my Phœbus!" she cried.

"Don't say his name. All of this is his fault— he was supposed to tell you that I was waiting for you. He let me pay him just so I could see you. You are a fool if you think he ever loved you."

"I don't believe you. He loved me. If he's not free, then I don't want to be free. And if he's dead, I don't care if I live. I will never forgive you for hurting him. All of this is your fault."

"The judge has decided to put you in the stocks after all, but I can help you. I can hide you in the church."

"No! If the stocks are to be my fate, then so be it. Leave now. I never want to see you again. Never!" She pushed him away and fell onto the filthy, wet floor.

# CHAPTER 14

# Sanctuary!

⌒

As it turned out, Captain Phœbus was not dead. His wounds had been serious, certainly, but they had healed. He had slipped away from the hospital one night after being questioned by Sir Robert, and had not returned.

He knew there would have to be a trial, and he wanted no part of it. Once he could stand up, he left to rejoin the army. But even being back there did not make him happy. Soon he wished to be back in Paris with Fleur-de-Lis, who now filled his heart. He'd had enough of silly girls, especially after one of them had almost gotten him killed.

Two months had passed by the time he arrived back at the home of Dame Aloise and her daughter.

The young lady was sitting by the window when he rode up on his horse. She flew downstairs to let him inside. She was very happy to see him.

"Where have you been?" she demanded.

"Oh, you are even more beautiful than the last time I saw you," Captain Phœbus replied, ignoring her question.

"Enough! Tell me, where have you been?" She pulled his arm and forced him inside. They went upstairs to the apartment.

"I was hurt and became ill."

"Hurt! What happened?"

"It was nothing really, just a scratch. A silly fight between men, that's all."

Fleur-de-Lis started to cry.

"Now, now," Phœbus said. "I'm fine, can't you see?"

"I'm just so glad you are well. I missed you! What was the fight about? Who did you quarrel with?"

Phœbus stood by the window. "Enough. It's done now. There is no need to relive it. Tell me, how are things in Paris? What's the latest news? Look at that crowd over there. What's happening?"

"I'm not sure. But I did hear that they were going to put a gypsy girl into the stocks today. Perhaps that's what the crowd is about."

"What is her name?" he asked absentmindedly.

"Does it really matter?" Fleur-de-Lis said.

"I suppose not," Phœbus replied, growing distracted as he looked at Fleur-de-Lis's pretty blond hair.

"Do you promise you'll never get hurt again?" she asked.

"I do."

"And you swear you love no one but me?"

"I do."

"Good," Fleur-de-Lis said. "Come, let's get some air."

She stepped onto the balcony, and Phœbus followed her.

The clock struck twelve. "There she is!" someone in the crowd called out.

"Why, it's that awful gypsy with the goat," Fleur-de-Lis said.

Phœbus turned very pale. "W-w-what?"

"You remember. The goat spelled out your name. Oh, it was terrible. Why are you so pale?" Fleur-de-Lis asked. "One would think you were shocked to see her there. What's wrong?"

"Nothing," Phœbus said quickly. "Nothing at all."

⁂

As they led Esmeralda through the square, she cried out for Phœbus. She looked around, and her eyes caught sight of Claude Frollo standing near the Rat Hole.

"Oh, no," she said. "Not him. He will haunt me even in my last moments."

Claude Frollo was pale. He was dressed in his official clothes, but looked very unhappy. He walked up to Esmeralda and said, "It's not too late. I can save you."

"I will never go with you. Go away or I will tell everyone it was you who attacked Phœbus, not me."

"They will never believe you."

"What have you done to him?" she cried.

"He is gone."

As the guards pulled her away, Esmeralda looked upward and saw him—Phœbus. He was there!

"Phœbus!" she cried. "Phœbus!" And with the shock of it all, Esmeralda fell to the ground.

In the confusion, no one noticed that Quasimodo had thrown a rope out the window of the bell tower. Just as the guards were about to pick Esmeralda up, he swung down, knocked them over, and grabbed her.

"Sanctuary!" he shouted. "Sanctuary!"

Quasimodo climbed back to the top of Notre-Dame and carried Esmeralda inside. He could see the crowd clapping and cheering. They loved Esmeralda so, and felt that she didn't deserve to be punished. Quasimodo had never been so proud in his entire life.

# CHAPTER 15

## Claude Frollo Grows Angry

$\backsim$

Claude Frollo needed time to think, so he left his official clothes behind and ordered a boatman to take him across the river.

Why had he attacked Captain Phœbus? What had the gypsy girl done to him? As he walked farther away from the center of Paris, bitter thoughts filled his mind. The captain was back! What was going to happen now? Now that Esmeralda was at Notre-Dame, exactly where he had wanted her all along!

⌒⌒

There were many places in Paris where a criminal could go to avoid being arrested. These were known as sanctuaries. The King's Guards were not allowed to enter them. They were the perfect place to hide. The only problem with a sanctuary was that the criminal could not leave.

There was a room in Notre-Dame that served as such a place. It was here that Quasimodo brought the gypsy girl after carrying her up the side of the church.

When she awoke, Esmeralda looked around. All kinds of thoughts rushed around her mind at once. She knew she was in Notre-Dame, and she knew that Quasimodo had helped her.

"Why did you save me?" she asked him. Quasimodo looked kindly at her and quietly left.

Esmeralda did not know what to do. She knew that Phœbus was alive—she had seen him — but he must no longer love her or else he would not leave her to her punishment like this.

Quasimodo knocked, and Esmeralda opened the door. But she couldn't say anything.

He handed her a basket of food and said, "It's okay. You're safe here. During the day you must stay in this room, but at night you can walk around the church. No one will know."

Before she could say anything, he left suddenly. Then something warm brushed her leg. It was Djali! Quasimodo had saved her, too. She cried and hugged her lovely little goat. When the sun went down, she left the safety of her small room.

❧

The next morning, Esmeralda woke to find Quasimodo looking in at her from the window.

"Oh!" she said, and waved at him. "Please, come in."

But because he could not hear her, Quasimodo thought she wanted him to go away.

"No, no!" She waved her hands again. "Come in, come in!" And so Quasimodo entered her room, and they stood there just looking at each other. She saw his one eye, his hunchback, and his crooked legs up close.

"I am deaf," he said at last.

Esmeralda nodded.

Quasimodo said, "You can speak to me with signs. And I can read your lips."

"Very well, then. Why did you save me?" she asked.

Quasimodo looked carefully at her pretty face. "I tried to carry you off that night, but you helped me the next day anyway. You gave me water. You were so kind." He stood up to leave, and she made a sign for him to stay.

"I must not. I have to work." He handed her a silver whistle. "You can call me with this—it's of a pitch I can still hear." And with that, he left her alone.

❧

Time passed. Esmeralda started to feel quite at home in her safe room. The bad memories of the past started to fade. She grew to love the sights and sounds of Notre-Dame. Like Quasimodo, the church became her whole world. The priests, the people who prayed, the walls, and especially the bells—they were her favorite. Quasimodo became a good friend. They spent a lot of time together. But one memory refused to go away: Phœbus. She cared for him more than ever.

One morning, Esmeralda was looking out her window. Quasimodo stood on the roof beside it. They were both watching the square.

Suddenly Esmeralda cried out, "Phœbus! Phœbus!"

Quasimodo saw that she was pointing at a handsome young officer on a horse down below. "Phœbus! Phœbus!" she called again. "He's going into that house. He doesn't hear me! Phœbus!"

"Shall I go and fetch him?" Quasimodo asked.

"Oh, please." She nodded and waved her arms. "Go quickly."

By the time Quasimodo made it to the square, the soldier was gone. He waved up to Esmeralda and motioned that he would wait until Phœbus came out of the house. Many people came and went—they were preparing for a celebration. The whole day passed this way: Quasimodo waiting, Esmeralda in the window, and Phœbus nowhere to be found.

Night fell. Candles were lit in the windows of the house. Quasimodo could see people dancing inside. Had he not been deaf, he would have heard the music, too.

It grew very late, but still Quasimodo waited. Great clouds hung in the dark sky and covered up the stars. Then, above him, two people came out on the balcony. It was Phœbus and Fleur-de-Lis. The captain had his arm around the girl. Seeing two happy and beautiful people made Quasimodo sad. He would never have that kind of life. He hoped Esmeralda couldn't see them, for he knew she would be upset.

Soon after, Quasimodo saw the captain leave the house and climb onto his horse. He raced past Quasimodo, but the hunchback ran after him and shouted, "Ho! Captain?"

Phœbus stopped and turned around. "What do you want with me?"

Quasimodo boldly took hold of the horse and said, "Follow me. There is someone who wants to talk to you."

"Wait! What are you doing? I know who you are—take your hands off my horse!"

Quasimodo did not hear him, and so he kept pulling the horse's reins toward Notre-Dame. In his rough voice, he said, "A woman who loves you is waiting."

The captain jumped down and stood in front of Quasimodo. "I know you are deaf, you silly fellow. Read my lips: I am to be married. Tell Esmeralda that—you are speaking of her, I presume. You are the hunchback who saved her, are you not? I want nothing to do with her."

Phœbus shook his head and jumped back on his horse. He pulled hard on the horse's reins, and Quasimodo fell to the ground. The captain galloped off into the night.

The hunchback stood up and brushed himself off. He did not follow them. Instead, he went back to the church.

"Did you find him?" Esmeralda asked.

"I did not," Quasimodo replied.

"You should have waited all night!" she shouted. "Go away, then. Just go."

Esmeralda was very unhappy with Quasimodo. He didn't want to upset her any more, so he stayed out of her way. When she woke each day, her breakfast was already there. One morning he left her a bunch of flowers. Esmeralda missed Quasimodo, but it was Phœbus she wanted to talk to. She spent hours watching the house across the street from her little window.

Meanwhile, Claude Frollo had shut his door to everyone. He locked himself away in his room with his books and potions. He would not even open the door for Jehan. He thought about Esmeralda day and night. One night his anger toward her boiled up so much that he put on his cloak, hung his keys from his waist, and left his secret hideaway.

*She has ruined my life,* Claude Frollo thought.

Esmeralda was asleep in her room. The sound of the door opening woke her, and she shut her eyes extra tight. *It must be the priest,* she thought. *Quasimodo would never enter my room without knocking.*

"Go away!" she yelled. "Get away from me!"

Claude Frollo grabbed her arms and said, "It's time for you to come with me. I am going to teach you a lesson. You have put a spell on me, you witch."

"No!" she shouted. "No!"

Djali bleated. Esmeralda pushed Claude Frollo away and blew hard on the silver whistle Quasimodo had given her. Suddenly Claude Frollo felt a very strong arm pull him away from the gypsy girl. It was Quasimodo! The two began to fight! Quasimodo did not realize that it was Claude Frollo until the moonlight shone on his face.

He stopped fighting instantly and said, "Claude Frollo, I am so sorry." The priest kicked

him once more, but by now they were in the hallway and Esmeralda had locked her door. Claude Frollo stumbled down the stairs. *This is not over,* he thought. *I will get her for what she done to me.*

Quasimodo's stomach hurt where Claude Frollo had kicked him. He stood up and held it tight. The whistle was on the floor outside of Esmeralda's room. He picked it up and knocked quietly on the door. "It's me, Quasimodo." Esmeralda opened the door and started to cry.

"Thank you," she said as she took the whistle. Then she threw herself on her bed and sobbed.

# CHAPTER 16

## Notre-Dame Under Attack

ᴄᴏ

Pierre had heard that Esmeralda was safe in Notre-Dame, and that made him happy. But he missed Djali. Life went on, however, and for the most part he thought no more about his "wife."

During the day, he performed tricks on the streets with the other tramps. At night, he wrote.

One day as he was walking down the street, a heavy hand fell on his shoulder. When he turned around, he saw Claude Frollo.

Pierre was shocked to see how pale his old

teacher had become. "How are you, Pierre?" Claude Frollo asked.

"So-so. My health is doing fine."

"You've had no trouble, then?"

"No, by my faith, none."

"Where are you going now?"

"Nowhere, really."

Then Claude Frollo asked the writer if he was happy, and Pierre said he was, very much so.

"But you are still poor?" Claude Frollo asked.

"Of course," Pierre answered.

Just then, Captain Phœbus and his company of King's Guards raced by on their horses. Claude Frollo stared coldly at the captain.

"Why do you glare so at that soldier?" Pierre asked.

"That is Captain Phœbus."

"Phœbus!" Pierre shouted. "That's the soldier who caused all the trouble with Esmeralda?"

"What do you know of her?"

Pierre looked strangely at Claude Frollo. "Nothing. I haven't seen her since the day of her trial when they were going to put her in the stocks."

"Is that all you know?"

"I heard she was taken into the sanctuary at Notre-Dame. But the courts have issued a decree that she is still to be punished. It's the first time they've done that—I heard it yesterday."

"What? What harm is it to have her stay at Notre-Dame?"

"They believe she should be punished for trying to kill Captain Phœbus. I heard, too, that the soldier said she was to blame. Quite amazing, how he disappeared and then came back."

"Don't you want to help her?"

"Oh, I am very busy with my books," Pierre replied.

"Yes, but can you think of nothing that could help her?" Claude Frollo asked.

"Well, we could try to get a pardon from Sir Robert."

"He would never agree." Claude Frollo paced back and forth. "There is only one way we can save her."

"Go on," Pierre said.

"We must smuggle her out of the city. She must pretend to be you, and you will pretend to be her. And then at the last minute, you can reveal who you really are."

"But they'll punish me instead!"

"Oh, they won't—you haven't done anything wrong."

Pierre hesitated. He didn't want to be punished. And he had so many things to do—walk the city, write his books—he didn't have time to be put in the stocks. "I don't think it's a good idea, but I will consider it."

Pierre looked at Claude Frollo. A tear fell down the priest's face.

"Fine, I will help," Pierre said. "But I've got a better idea."

"Well . . ." Claude Frollo started.

"The tramps—my friends—they'll save her. She's a favorite among them. Here's the plan." He whispered into Claude Frollo's ear.

When he finished, Claude Frollo shook Pierre's hand and said, "Yes, that will work."

Claude Frollo returned to Notre-Dame and found Jehan waiting for him. "Brother," he said, "I have come to see you."

"What is it?" Claude Frollo asked without looking up at him.

"I need more advice. You see, you are—were—right about school and studying."

"And?"

"I have been very bad, involved in folly, and made a fool of myself. I owe everyone money. I want to lead a better life."

"You do?"

"Yes, but I need a little money first."

"I have none to give."

"Truly?" Jehan asked.

"Truly," Claude Frollo answered.

"Well then," Jehan said, "I shall become a tramp."

Claude Frollo looked at him coldly. "Fine."

Jehan made a little bow and left the room. Claude Frollo watched him from the window. Just as he was about to leave the garden, he threw down a purse.

"That is the last money you shall have from me!"

Jehan smiled and went on his way.

⌒

Pierre sat in the corner of the dark room, surrounded by the tramps. There was a big party going on. People were everywhere, dancing and singing.

"Hurrah! Hurrah!" someone called out, "I am a tramp!" It was Jehan. "I was a gentleman, but now I am one of you! And this is our plan tonight. We are to go to Notre-Dame and save the girl! Burn the place down! My fortune is gone, and so I join all you great men and women. We must save Esmeralda!"

A woman handed Jehan his dinner. He sat down and started to eat, forgetting his speech at once. In the distance, the church bells rang.

The beggar Clopin stood up and said, "That's it! Notre-Dame's bells are ringing—it's time for us to go."

The band of tramps left their warm room and walked along winding streets of Paris toward Notre-Dame.

⁓

Quasimodo couldn't sleep after he rang the midnight bells, so he went upstairs and sat on top of the north tower. It was very dark. The only light came from the gate of Saint Antoine.

Strange things had been happening recently. Over the past few days, Quasimodo had seen men looking up at Esmeralda's window. And Claude Frollo had been acting even odder than usual.

Suddenly Quasimodo noticed that the black line of the water seemed taller than normal. He looked harder. There were heads! It was a crowd. And they were moving toward the church. The long line of people was silent. They looked like a fog, slowly creeping forward.

*Esmeralda!* he thought. *They must be coming for her.*

Quasimodo knew he had to stop them. The crowd grew nearer. They were carrying sticks and other weapons. They stopped in front of the church and lit their torches. Quasimodo knew some of the faces—the men and women who had crowned him the Pope of Fools.

The tramps had taken their places around the

church. Even Jehan was there. Clopin gave the order. "The courts want to punish Esmeralda even though she has claimed the safety of the church! We need to save her. Let's go!"

The men moved up the stairs and tried to pry open the door. They pushed and pushed, but it would not budge.

Then a giant beam fell from the top of the church and crashed to the ground. The tramps were scared, and many of them ran away. They didn't know what had happened—some thought it was magic.

"Get up men! To the door!" Clopin said. "Let's go!"

The men looked at the beam and up at the church. They didn't move. They were too scared.

"It's just a piece of wood!" Clopin called. "Nothing to be afraid of!"

"Let's use it to break down the door!" Jehan cried.

"Hurrah!" the tramps cried as they bashed the beam against the door. The door made a sound like a big drum. But it didn't break. They hit it again.

Then a shower of stones fell onto the tramps from above. It was Quasimodo—he was defending Notre-Dame!

The hunchback knew the door wouldn't hold for long. The tramps hit the door one more time and heard a giant bang behind them.

"What was that?" one of them cried.

"It's more magic!" another one shouted.

"Let's go! This isn't worth our lives!"

Giant explosions came from the roof—lighting up all of the sculptures on the side of the church and making them seem alive. Quasimodo was lighting firecrackers!

"What happened to everyone?" Clopin asked when he looked around. "Where did they all go?"

"The magic scared them off!" one of the tramps answered.

"Where is Pierre? Has he run off, too, the coward? And what about Jehan? Is he also gone? Come on, men. What will happen to Esmeralda if we don't save her?"

Jehan walked toward them carrying a ladder. "Let's use this!" he cried. Somehow he had found a strange metal helmet and wore it on his head.

"What are you going to do with that?" Clopin asked him.

"Do you see that window up there?" Clopin nodded. "I am going to use the ladder to get inside. From that hallway I can get into the church."

In an instant the ladder was up against the wall of the cathedral. Jehan started up slowly. He had just made it inside the gallery when Quasimodo appeared. The hunchback groaned as he pushed the ladder off the wall. When it landed on the ground, it broke in half. No one else would be able to use it. Jehan was inside by himself with

Quasimodo, who grabbed him, held him tight,
and then tied him up.

Pierre was having a bad night indeed. As he tried
to get to the tramps near the church, one of the
King's Guards pulled him inside the Great Hall,
where Sir Robert was waiting.

The guard said, "Here is one of the tramps that
are attacking the city."

"Who are you and what are you doing?" Sir
Robert asked.

Pierre hung his head. "I am Pierre Gringoire. I
am a poet, and this has all been one big mistake."

"Take him to jail!" Sir Robert shouted.

"No! Wait . . ." Pierre started to explain that he
was a very loyal citizen of Paris and not really a
tramp at all.

"Oh, I recognize you now. You were the man who wrote the play during the Festival of Fools," Sir Robert said. "Let him go—he's not one of the troublemakers."

As the guards were throwing Pierre back into the street, another guard arrived. "Sir Robert," he said, "the crowd is attacking Notre-Dame. They are trying to save the gypsy girl."

Sir Robert thought for a minute and then ordered everyone out to fight the crowd. "Make sure you take Captain Phœbus's guards with you," he added. "They are the best we have."

Pierre stumbled down the street until he came to a stop in front of a man in a black cloak. "Is that you, Claude Frollo?"

"You are late, as always, Pierre."

"It's not my fault. I was arrested by the King's Guards."

"I don't care. What is the password of the tramps? Without the secret word, they won't let me near them," Claude Frollo said. "Tell me now!"

"Oh, oh, it is, um, *petite flambé en Bastille.* Yes, that's it."

"Good, now they will let us pass. They've blocked up all the streets, those tramps. I've got a key to the towers that will let us into the church. Let's go!"

And so the two men raced down the street in the direction of Notre-Dame.

༄

Quasimodo looked outside and saw the crowd growing even angrier. He didn't know what to do.

He was about to give up the cause entirely when he saw Captain Phœbus and his men. A great fight broke out between his company and the tramps — but the soldiers were stronger. It was a fearful sight. The church and Esmeralda were safe! But when Quasimodo ran down the hallway and into her room, it was empty. She was gone!

# CHAPTER 17

# An Unhappy Reunion

⟶⟵

Esmeralda woke to find two men in her room. She screamed, and one said, "Don't worry, it's me, Pierre!

"You are in danger," he continued. "The mob is coming to save you—they are going to destroy the church. You could be hurt."

"Who is that man with you?" she asked as she gathered her shawl around her.

"Just a friend. Come on!"

The three of them and Djali raced down the tower steps and out into the churchyard. They took back alleys until they reached the water, where a small boat was waiting for them.

As they began to row away, Pierre could not hold back his excitement. "We have escaped! You are safe!" he said. The strange man in the cloak, who was really Claude Frollo, said nothing.

Esmeralda looked at him. He scared her with his scowl and dark hood. She didn't know he was the priest. He rowed on and on and didn't say a word. Pierre meanwhile happily chatted away as the boat moved down the river.

The boat bumped when it reached the shore. The man in the cloak offered Esmeralda his hand to help her out of the boat, but she did not take it—something about him made her very uneasy.

Pierre was already on the shore with Djali.

*I cannot save them both,* he thought. *She'll be fine here with Claude Frollo. I'm going to make my own way.* And with that, he took Djali by the collar and fled.

When Esmeralda got out of the boat, she

noticed that both Djali and Pierre were gone. She was alone with the strange man! She shivered as he grabbed her hand and pulled her along behind him. They made their way to the Place de Grève.

The man stopped in front of the stocks and lifted up his hood to reveal his face. "This is where they will put you if they catch you. I am going to give you a choice. You can go with me and be safe. I will love you. Or you can be humiliated there for days."

"I knew it was you!" Esmeralda cried. "Never! I will never go with you. You are a terrible man!" she shouted at him. "I will always love Phœbus and only Phœbus."

"Then I can no longer help you. Sack Woman, here is your gypsy. Have your revenge!" he said and raced away into the night.

Esmeralda felt a cold hand grab her wrist. She pulled and pulled, but could not get away. "What have I done to you?" she cried.

"They stole my child, the gypsies. This is what you have done to me."

"But I was not even born then," Esmeralda said.

"Oh, yes, you must have been born then. She would be about your age. Fifteen years I have suffered. Now it is your turn, you evil girl!"

"Please, let me go. Please, I am just an orphan girl who looks for her parents. We are not so different. You lost a child—I lost my mother and father."

"You took my baby. All I have left of her is this shoe." The Sack Woman, Paquette, took out the tiny embroidered shoe.

"What?" Esmeralda said. "It can't be . . ." She pulled off the necklace she wore around her neck and opened the small pouch. The other shoe was inside!

"Agnes?" the old woman said and started to cry. "Agnes!"

"Mother?" Esmeralda said. "Is it really you?"

They hugged each other for a very long time. Suddenly they heard a loud noise. It was the soldiers.

"Quickly," Paquette said. "We must hide. We're not safe here in the square."

They slipped back inside the dark Rat Hole. "Hide in the corner—they won't look for you there."

Esmeralda bent down, and Paquette looked out the barred window.

"This way, Captain Phœbus!" one of the soldiers cried. "The old woman in the Rat Hole— that's what the priest said—it's over here."

Esmeralda tried to stand up when she heard his name. "Stay down," Paquette hissed, "or they will find you!"

The soldiers were there in a heartbeat. "Old woman," one said, "we're looking for a gypsy. We were told that you had her. Where is she?"

"I do not know. She ran away."

"Which way did she go, old woman, which way?"

"She ran toward the river—I think she's trying to escape by water."

The soldiers raced off to look for Esmeralda by the riverbank.

"It's safe," Paquette whispered.

Esmeralda stood up from the corner. Then, from outside, she heard a voice so lovely that she ran out of the Rat Hole before Paquette could stop her. "Phœbus! Phœbus, please, come here!"

But Phœbus did not hear Esmeralda cry out to him. He was already gone. The only man left was a soldier she didn't know. Esmeralda tried to run after Phœbus.

"Stop!" the soldier called. "Stop now, prisoner, or else I will have to hurt you!"

Esmeralda raced away as fast as she could.

# CHAPTER 18

## Quasimodo Is Too Late

～

After seeing her empty room, Quasimodo ran
out of Notre-Dame and into the streets to find
Esmeralda. He raced to the Place de Grève, but
he was too late. Esmeralda was dead. The soldier
had caught her on his horse, but they had strug-
gled, and she had fallen to her death on the
cobblestones.

In his heart, Quasimodo knew that Claude
Frollo was to blame—all of this was the arch-
deacon's fault. Quasimodo raced back to Notre-
Dame, but again, he was too late. Claude

Frollo's things were gone — his room ransacked. Quasimodo knew that the priest had run away in shame.

Quasimodo cried and cried. And then he, too, sped off into the night. And to this day, no one knows whatever became of the hunchback of Notre-Dame.

# What Do *You* Think?
## Questions for Discussion

᷈

Have you ever been around a toddler who keeps asking the question "Why?" Does your teacher call on you in class with questions from your homework? Do your parents ask you questions about your day at the dinner table? We are always surrounded by questions that need a specific response. But is it possible to have a question with no right answer?

The following questions are about the book you just read. But this is not a quiz! They are designed to help you look at the people, places, and events in the story from different angles. These questions do not have specific answers. Instead, they might make you think of the story in a completely new way.

Think carefully about each question and enjoy discovering more about this classic story.

1. Why is Pierre so angry at the people watching his play? Have you ever been interrupted while you were trying to do something important? How did you react?

2. How does Quasimodo react when the students begin to tease him? Has anyone ever made fun of you? What did you do?

3. How does Pierre try to prove that he's a tramp? Did you think he would succeed? What is the hardest thing you've ever tried to do?

4. Claude Frollo says that he wanted to be a priest ever since he was a little boy. What do you want to be when you grow up?

5. Why does Quasimodo look up to Claude Frollo as he does? Do you think this is wise? Who is your role model?

6. Why does Quasimodo rescue Esmeralda? Have you ever helped someone who couldn't help him or herself?

7. How does Pacquette react when she hears Eustache's voice? Do you think she is right to blame Esmeralda for her problems?

8. What does Esmeralda promise her gypsy parents? Why does she decide to break her promise? Have you ever broken a promise to someone?

9. Why doesn't Pierre want to help Esmeralda avoid the stocks? Do you think he is right to worry? Have you ever been punished for something you didn't do?

10. What do you think happens to Quasimodo? Where would you go if you had to get away from everyone?

# Afterword

*by Arthur Pober, Ed.D.*

∽

First impressions are important.

Whether we are meeting new people, going to new places, or picking up a book unknown to us, first impressions count for a lot. They can lead to warm, lasting memories or can make us shy away from any future encounters.

Can you recall your own first impressions and earliest memories of reading the classics?

Do you remember wading through pages and pages of text to prepare for an exam? Or were you the child who hid under the blanket to read with a flashlight, joining forces with Robin Hood to save Maid Marian? Do you remember only how long it took you to read a lengthy novel such as *Little Women*? Or did you become best friends with the March sisters?

Even for a gifted young reader, getting through long chapters with dense language can easily become overwhelming and can obscure the richness of the story and its characters. Reading an abridged, newly crafted version of a classic novel can be the gentle introduction a child needs to explore the characters and storyline without the frustration of difficult vocabulary and complex themes.

Reading an abridged version of a classic novel gives the young reader a sense of independence and the satisfaction of finishing a "grown-up" book. And when a child is engaged with and inspired by a classic story, the tone is set for further exploration of the story's themes, characters, history, and details. As a child's reading skills advance, the desire to tackle the original, unabridged version of the story will naturally emerge.

If made accessible to young readers, these stories can become invaluable tools for understanding themselves in the context of their families and social environments. This is why the Classic Starts series includes questions that stimulate discussion regarding the impact and social relevance of the characters and stories today. These questions can foster lively conversations between children and their parents or teachers. When we look at the issues, values, and standards of past times in terms of how we live now, we can appreciate literature's classic tales in a very personal and engaging way.

Share your love of reading the classics with a young child, and introduce an imaginary world real enough to last a lifetime.

## Dr. Arthur Pober, Ed.D.

Dr. Arthur Pober has spent more than twenty years in the fields of early childhood and gifted education. He is the former principal of one of the world's oldest laboratory schools for gifted youngsters, Hunter College Elementary School, and former Director of Magnet Schools for the Gifted and Talented for more than 25,000 youngsters in New York City.

Dr. Pober is a recognized authority in the areas of media and child protection and is currently the U.S. representative to the European Institute for the Media and European Advertising Standards Alliance.

Explore these wonderful stories in our
Classic Starts™ library.

*20,000 Leagues Under the Sea*

*The Adventures of Huckleberry Finn*

*The Adventures of Robin Hood*

*The Adventures of Sherlock Holmes*

*The Adventures of Tom Sawyer*

*Anne of Green Gables*

*Arabian Nights*

*Around the World in 80 Days*

*Black Beauty*

*The Call of the Wild*

*Dracula*

*Frankenstein*

*Gulliver's Travels*

*Heidi*

*The Hunchback of Notre-Dame*